Blue-Ribbon Bunny

Based on the episode written by Craig Gerber

Adapted by Sarah Nathan

Illustrated by Character Building Studio
and the Disney Storybook Art Team

DISNEP PRESS

New York • Los Angeles

First Edition 10 9 8 7 6 5 4 3 2
ISBN 978-1-4231-7158-4

G658-7729-4-14161

Manufactured in the USA
For more Disney Press fun, visit www.disneybooks.com

SUSTAINABLE
FORESTRY
INITIATIVE

Certified Chain of Custody
Promoting Sustainable Forestry

www.sfiprogram.org
SFI-01415

The SFI label applies to the text stock

The fair is in town!
There is a pet contest.

"I wish I had a pet," Sofia says.

"What about your pet bunny?"
James asks.
"Clover is my friend," says Sofia.
"He is not a pet."

Sofia wants a blue ribbon.
The winner gets to be in the parade.

Maybe Clover will
be in the contest!

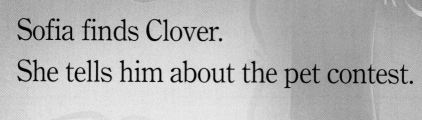

Sofia finds Clover.
She tells him about the pet contest.

Clover says he will be Sofia's pet.
"I am a blue-ribbon bunny!"

Amber and James are in the garden.
Their pets are doing tricks.

Not Clover.
He wants to eat carrots.

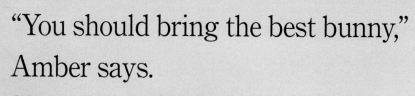

"You should bring the best bunny," Amber says.

She takes Sofia to the castle zoo.

Sofia meets Ginger.
Her fur is white as snow.
Ginger can whistle, too!

"I am bringing Clover," Sofia says.

Sofia's friends practice.

Prince Zandar rides his elephant.

Princess Vivian brings her dragon.

Hildegard brings her mink.
Each pet is special.

"Are you special?" Sofia asks.

"I can dance," Clover says.

Sofia wants Clover to look special.
"No way!" he says.

Sofia wants the blue ribbon.
She wants to ride in the parade.

"I can take another bunny,"
she says.

"Fine," says Clover.
"I can take a nap."

Sofia goes to the castle zoo.
Ginger will be her pet.
Ginger loves bows!

Crackle the dragon sees Clover.
"Are you in the pet contest?"

"I am not a blue-ribbon bunny,"
Clover says sadly.

Sofia and Ginger get ready.
"This is going to be fun," says Sofia.

"Pet contests are serious,"
Ginger says.

Sofia spots blueberries!
"Here! Catch!" she says.

"No," says Ginger.

Crackle calls to Sofia.

"You hurt Clover's feelings!"

"He didn't want to come," Sofia says.

"Yes, he did," says Crackle.

A boy runs by with his dog.
"How long have you had your pet?"
he asks.

Sofia looks sad. "Not long."

"I've had Max since he was a pup," the boy says. "He is my best friend."

Sofia thinks of Clover.

"I made a mistake," she says.

"I want to be with my friend."

Sofia finds Clover.

"You are so special to me," she says.

"You are my best friend!"

Clover is happy. "I want to win
the blue ribbon!" he says.

Sofia and Clover go to the fair.
Clover does his dance. He is great!
They are having fun.

Who will win the contest?

"The best pet is . . . Clover!"

Everyone cheers.

Sofia turns to Clover on the float.
"I have treats for you at home."
"You do?" asks Clover.
"Treats for my blue-ribbon bunny!"